Published by Grolier Direct Marketing, Danbury, Connecticut

Printed in the U.S.A.

ISBN 0-7172-8329-1

JIM HENSON'S MUPPETS

IN

# Nobody's Perfect

## A Book About Making Mistakes

By Stephanie St. Pierre • Illustrated by Joe Ewers

GROLIER

It was Monday night—and Gonzo's turn to help with the dinner dishes. After everything was dried, Gonzo stacked the pots and pans into a tall tower.

Gonzo was very proud of his tower. It was so high, he had to use a step stool to reach the top.

"Hey, everybody," Gonzo said, pointing to the pile of pots. "Ta-da!"

"Oh, Gonzo, be careful," cried his grandmother. But it was too late. *Crash!* went the pots and pans, right into the bowl of popcorn-and-prune pudding his grandmother was going to serve for dessert!

Gonzo felt bad. "Sorry, Grandma," he said.

Gonzo was glad his grandmother wasn't mad. But nobody got dessert that night. And nobody thought his tower was so wonderful.

Unfortunately, Gonzo moved a little too fast, and Mr. Robot banged right into the jar Piggy was holding.

"Eeek!" Piggy cried.

"Bzzzz! Boink! Whirr!" went Mr. Robot.

*Crash!* went Piggy's jar. It hit the ground and shattered.

“Oh, no,” said Piggy. Everyone watched in amazement as five orange butterflies flew away from the broken jar. “My project is ruined,” wailed Piggy.

Gonzo felt terrible all day long. He offered to share his project with Piggy, but she just shook her head.

"Uh-oh, I really messed up this time," Gonzo said to himself glumly.

Piggy was still mad on Wednesday. Gonzo tried to make her feel better at lunchtime by balancing some peanut-butter-and-baloney sandwiches on his feet. But Piggy didn't laugh.

Then one of Gonzo's feet knocked over Fozzie's milk. The lunch lady didn't laugh, either.

On Thursday, Gonzo couldn't stop thinking about how many things had gone wrong that week. He was beginning to think he couldn't do anything right at all.

As usual, on the way home from school that day, Gonzo was collecting interesting junk. When he found a sparkling blue stone, he thought of Piggy. Maybe this would make her feel better!

“Hey, Gonzo!” Scooter and Skeeter called from across the street. “We’re going to the clubhouse. Do you want to come?”

“Yeah, sure,” said Gonzo. He put the things he’d collected in a pile by the curb and hurried after his friends.

As he entered the clubhouse, Gonzo tripped. “Whoa,” he said.

“Are you okay?” Scooter asked.

“I can’t seem to do anything right,” Gonzo moaned, shaking his head. “I’m just a big goof-up.” Gonzo told his friends about all of the mistakes he’d made during the week. “I’m afraid to do anything at all. I don’t know what I’ll mess up next.” He looked sadly out the window.

"Oh, no!" he cried, pointing outside. There was the garbage truck across the street, collecting the trash...including Gonzo's junk!

"Yikes!" Gonzo shouted. "My present for Piggy is in that truck." Gonzo got up and ran after the truck. "Wait!" he called. "Wait!" But it was too late. Soon the truck was far away.

On Friday, Gonzo moped around all day long. By then, everybody had begun worrying about him.

"What's the matter with Gonzo?" Piggy asked Scooter and Skeeter. They told her about the garbage truck and the cheer-up present Gonzo had lost.

Suddenly, Piggy felt bad for Gonzo. She went to talk to him.

“Hi, Gonzo,” Piggy said. “I heard about the present you almost gave me.”

“Yeah, I messed *that* up, too,” sighed Gonzo.

“Well, nobody’s perfect, Gonzo,” said Piggy. “Everybody makes mistakes. Even *I* do, sometimes.”

"Like when?" wondered Gonzo.

"Well, my mother told me not to use a glass jar for my science project. She gave me a plastic one, but it wasn't pretty so I used the glass jar. Then it fell, and that was the end of my science project. So it was my mistake, too."

Gonzo thought for a minute. "I guess mistakes happen to everybody," he said.

Looking down, Gonzo noticed a caterpillar on the ground. "Hey, look," he said, holding it out to Piggy. "Someday this will be a butterfly. Then you can start a new science project."

"Right. And this time, I won't use a glass jar," laughed Piggy.

"Perfect!" said Gonzo.

## Let's Talk About Making Mistakes

There isn't anybody in the world who doesn't make mistakes. Whether they're little ones or big ones, there is something we can learn from each mistake we make. For instance, in this book, Gonzo learns that making mistakes doesn't make you a bad person. A mistake is not the end of the world.

Here are some questions about making mistakes for you to think about:

What's a mistake that you especially remember making? What happened after you made that mistake?

What do you think you have learned from your mistakes?

What are some good things to do after you make a mistake?